Ricky Ricotta's Mighty Robot Adventures

VOLUME 2

Three More Adventures by

DAV PILKEY

Pictures by

MARTIN ONTIVEROS

SCHOLASTIC INC.

New York Toronto London Auckland Sydney
Mexico City New Delhi Hong Kong Buenos Aires

D1468848

Ricky Ricotta's Mighty Robot vs. the Mecha-Monkeys from Mars, text copyright © 2002 by Dav Pilkey, illustrations copyright © 2002 by Martin Ontiveros. Originally published in hardcover by the Blue Sky Press in 2002.

Ricky Ricotta's Mighty Robot vs. the Jurassic Jackrabbits from Jupiter, text copyright © 2002 by Dav Pilkey, illustrations copyright © 2002 by Martin Ontiveros. Originally published in hardcover by the Blue Sky Press in 2002.

Ricky Ricotta's Mighty Robot vs. the Stupid Stinkbugs from Saturn, text copyright © 2003 by Dav Pilkey, illustrations copyright © 2003 by Martin Ontiveros. Originally published in hardcover by the Blue Sky Press in 2003.

12 11 10 9 8 7 6 5 4 3 2 1   6 7 8 9 10 11/0

Printed in the United States of America   40

This edition created exclusively for Barnes & Noble, Inc.
2006 Barnes & Noble Books

ISBN-13: 978-0-7607-9637-5

ISBN-10: 0-7607-9637-8

First compilation printing, October 2006

CONTENTS

Ricky Ricotta's Mighty Robot vs. the Mecha-Monkeys from Mars

For Felix

—D. P.

To Felix Salvador Ontiveros:

I can't wait to read this one to you!

—M. O.

Chapters

CHAPTER 1

The Big Mistake

One day, Ricky Ricotta
and his Mighty Robot were
playing hide-and-seek
in their yard.

"This game is too easy," said Ricky.
"Let's ride skateboards instead!"

Ricky got his skateboard out of the
garage, but there was no skateboard
big enough for his Mighty Robot.

"I know," said Ricky. "We can
use my parents' minivan!"

Soon, Ricky and his Mighty Robot
were zooming down the street.
"This is fun!" said Ricky.

FONDUE
POND 1 MILE

But it stopped being fun
when they wiped out.
CRASH!

SPLASH!!!

When Ricky and his Robot
got out of the pond, they saw
the smashed-up minivan.

Ricky's Mighty Robot put the
minivan back in the driveway.
"Maybe Mom and Dad won't
notice," said Ricky.

But they did.

CHAPTER 2

Big Trouble

Ricky's mother and father were not happy.

"Alright," said Ricky's father. "Which one of you boys squished our minivan?"

Ricky and his Mighty Robot
looked down at the ground.
They were very worried.

Finally, Ricky confessed.

"We both did," said Ricky.

"It was an accident."

"You boys were very irresponsible," said Ricky's father.

"Yes," said Ricky's mother, "and you will have to find a way to pay for the damage you have done."

CHAPTER 3
Major Monkey Hates Mars

Meanwhile, about 35 million miles away on the planet Mars, there lived a mean little monkey who was hatching an evil plan.

His name was Major Monkey,
and he hated living on Mars.
Mars was a cold, dry, and
very, very lonely place.

Major Monkey kept himself busy by building evil Robots and strange machines in his secret laboratory, but he was still lonely.

There was nobody to talk to. There
was nobody to yell at . . . and, worst
of all, there was nobody to be mean to.
So Major Monkey decided to take
over the planet Earth and enslave all
of mousekind.

Major Monkey had watched Earth for many months. He saw other evil villains try to take over the planet, but they were always stopped by Ricky Ricotta's Mighty Robot.

"I must get rid of that Mighty Robot!" said Major Monkey. "And I know just how to do it."

CHAPTER 4

The Trap

The next morning, as Ricky and his Mighty Robot walked to school, they tried to think of a way to pay for their mistake of wrecking the minivan.

"How many years will it take to buy a new minivan with my allowance?" asked Ricky.

Ricky's Robot used his super
brain to figure out the answer.
"Hmmm," said Ricky. "Only
259 years? Maybe we should
think of a better plan."

Suddenly, a small spaceship
zoomed out of the sky. The top
of the spaceship opened up,
and a spacemouse peeked out.

"Help us! Help us!" cried
the spacemouse. "Mars is
under attack! We need your
Mighty Robot to save us!"

Ricky Ricotta's Mighty Robot could not turn away from someone who needed help. So the Mighty Robot followed the tiny spaceship all the way to Mars.

"Be careful up there!"
Ricky shouted.

CHAPTER 5

Betrayed

Ricky's Mighty Robot soon arrived on Mars. He saw a strange laboratory, but he did not see any evil villains.

The Mighty Robot flew closer to the laboratory. Suddenly, a giant metal hand reached out of the hillside.

41

It grabbed Ricky's Robot and would not let go.

Ricky's Mighty Robot tried and tried, but he could not escape the grip of the giant metal hand.

Major Monkey looked up from
the tiny spaceship and pulled
a puppet off his hand.

"I tricked you! I tricked you!"
Major Monkey mocked. "Now
it is *YOU* who needs help!
Haw-haw-haw!"

Major Monkey pressed a button inside his spaceship. Soon, three giant Mecha-Monkeys rose from the depths of the strange laboratory.

Major Monkey called out to his troops: "Mecha-Monkeys!" he cried. "It is time to take over Earth. Follow ME!"

CHAPTER 6

Major Monkey Makes His Move

Ricky was taking a spelling test when he saw the little spaceship return with three enormous Mecha-Monkeys.

"Hey," cried Ricky, "where's
my Robot?"

"He got into a tight squeeze,"
laughed Major Monkey. "And
he's never coming BACK—
haw-haw-haw!"

"NOOOOO!" cried Ricky. But there was nothing he could do.

Major Monkey flew through the
streets of Squeakyville and ordered
everyone on Earth to surrender.

CHAPTER 7

The Mouse from S.A.S.A.

That afternoon, Ricky sat in his bedroom missing his best friend.

"We are sure that your Robot will be O.K.," said Ricky's mother.

"Yes," said Ricky's father. "He'll find a way to escape. I just know it."

Soon, there was a knock on
the front door. It was a general
from the Squeakyville Air and
Space Association.

"We are going to send a space shuttle up to Mars to rescue your Mighty Robot," said the general. "He is our only hope."

"Hooray!" cried Ricky.

"And we need you to come
with us, Ricky," said the general.
"You know that Robot better
than anybody."

"Can I go?" Ricky asked his
parents. "Pleeeeease?"

"Well," said Ricky's father, "alright. But you must promise to be careful!"

"Hooray!" cried Ricky.

CHAPTER 8

The Space Shuttle

Ricky and his parents got into the general's car. The general turned on the rocket boosters, and they all flew straight to the Space Center.

"This is *so cool*!" said Ricky's father.

Soon, Ricky was sitting inside a giant space shuttle with three real astro-mice.

Ricky fastened his seat
belt, and off they blasted
into outer space.

When the shuttle arrived on
Mars, Ricky and the astro-mice
saw Major Monkey's laboratory.

They saw the Mighty Robot trapped inside the giant metal hand. But what could they do?

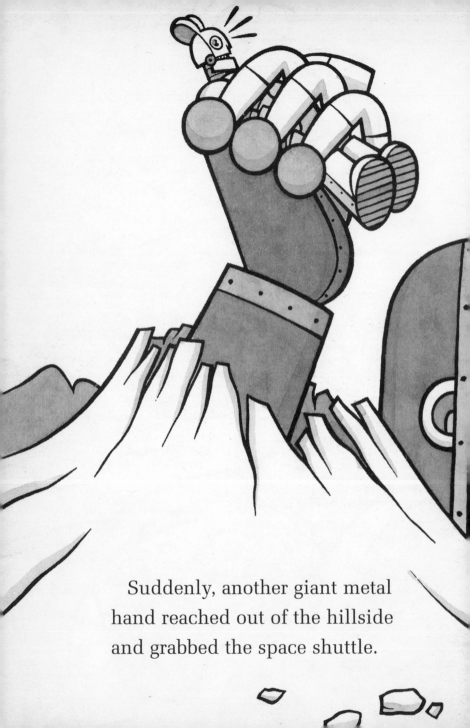

Suddenly, another giant metal
hand reached out of the hillside
and grabbed the space shuttle.

Then the strange laboratory
began to rise from the ground.

It rose higher and higher . . .

. . . until finally it stepped out of the ground. Major Monkey's laboratory had turned into a colossal Orangu-Tron.

The astro-mice inside the space shuttle tried to open the emergency exit door, but it was stuck. It could only open halfway.

"I think I can fit through," said Ricky.

Ricky squeezed his way out of the space shuttle and headed toward the laboratory.

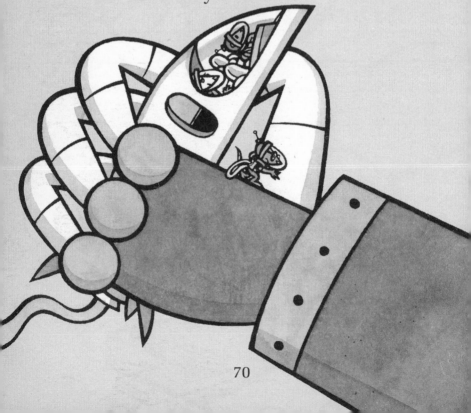

CHAPTER 9

Ricky to the Rescue

The Orangu-Tron stomped its feet as Ricky bravely climbed up its giant arm.

Soon, Ricky found a doorway
in the Orangu-Tron's ear, and he
crawled inside the strange laboratory.

Once inside, Ricky looked around
the control center. He saw lots of evil
Robots and many strange machines.

73

Then, Ricky found the main power switch.

Ricky grabbed the switch and tried to turn off the power, but the switch was stuck. Ricky pulled and pulled on the switch.

ORANGU-TRON MAIN POWER SWITCH

Finally, Ricky was spotted by an
evil Robo-Chimp.

"Destroy the intruder!" said the
Robo-Chimp. "Destroy the intruder!"

The Robo-Chimp grabbed Ricky's
breathing tube and started pulling.
Soon, other Robo-Chimps joined
in. Harder and harder they pulled.

Then Ricky got an idea. He wrapped his breathing tube around the main power switch and held on tight. The Robo-Chimps pulled and pulled. Finally, the switch began to move.

The harder the Robo-Chimps
pulled, the more the switch moved.

Ka-KLANK!

Suddenly, the power for the
whole laboratory turned off.

"Hooray!" cried Ricky.

CHAPTER 10

Freedom

Outside, the Orangu-Tron lost all of its power. Ricky's Mighty Robot pushed his way out of the giant metal hand. He was free at last!

But inside, Ricky was in trouble.
The Robo-Chimps rushed toward
Ricky. "Must destroy intruder!" they
chanted. "Must restore power!"

"HELP ME!" screamed Ricky
as the Robo-Chimps came
closer and closer.

81

KER-POW!
Ricky's Mighty Robot
punched a hole in the roof and
grabbed Ricky just in time.

82

Ricky pushed the SELF-DESTRUCT
button with his tail. "Let's get out of
here!" cried Ricky as the laboratory
began to shake and crumble.

With Ricky in one hand and the
space shuttle in the other, Ricky's
Mighty Robot zoomed into space—
just in time.

KA-BOOOOOOOOM!

"That takes care of Mars,"
said Ricky. "Now we have to
save Earth!"

CHAPTER 11

Back to Earth

When they got back to Earth,
Ricky's Mighty Robot spotted
Major Monkey.

"What—what are *YOU* doing
here?" asked Major Monkey.
"We're here to save Earth!"
said Ricky.

"Oh, yeah?" said Major Monkey.
"We'll see about that!" He called his
Mecha-Monkeys and ordered them
to destroy Ricky's Mighty Robot.

Ricky's Robot put Ricky and
the space shuttle someplace safe.
Then the robo-battle began.

Ricky's Robot treated
the Mecha-Monkeys to
two servings of *punch* . . .

. . . and a *knuckle sandwich*.

Major Monkey was very upset. "Alright, banana brains," he shouted. "Quit monkeying around! Let's see some action!"

CHAPTER 12

The Big Battle

(IN FLIP-O-RAMA™)

Hey, kids!
You can animate
the action by following
these easy steps!

D-RaMa

HERE'S HOW IT WORKS!

STEP 1
Place your *left* hand inside the dotted lines marked "LEFT HAND HERE." Hold the book open *flat*.

STEP 2
Grasp the *right-hand* page with your right thumb and index finger (inside the dotted lines marked "RIGHT THUMB HERE").

STEP 3
Now *quickly* flip the right-hand page back and forth until the picture appears to be *animated*.

(For extra fun, try adding your own sound-effects!)

FLIP-O-RAMA 1

(pages 101 and 103)

Remember, flip *only* page 101.
While you are flipping, be sure
you can see the picture on page 101
and the one on page 103.
If you flip quickly, the two
pictures will start to look like
<u>one</u> *animated* picture.

Don't forget to add
your own sound-effects!

LEFT HAND HERE

The Mecha-Monkeys
Attacked.

RIGHT
THUMB
HERE

The Mecha-Monkeys
Attacked.

FLIP-O-RAMA 2

(pages 105 and 107)

Remember, flip *only* page 105.
While you are flipping, be sure
you can see the picture on page 105
and the one on page 107.
If you flip quickly, the two
pictures will start to look like
<u>one</u> *animated* picture.

Don't forget to add
your own sound-effects!

LEFT HAND HERE

Ricky's Robot
Fought Back.

RIGHT
THUMB
HERE

Ricky's Robot
Fought Back.

FLIP-O-RAMA 3

(pages 109 and 111)

Remember, flip *only* page 109.
While you are flipping, be sure
you can see the picture on page 109
and the one on page 111.
If you flip quickly, the two
pictures will start to look like
<u>one</u> *animated* picture.

Don't forget to add
your own sound-effects!

LEFT HAND HERE

The Mecha-Monkeys Battled Hard.

RIGHT THUMB HERE

The Mecha-Monkeys
Battled Hard.

FLIP-O-RAMA 4

(pages 113 and 115)

Remember, flip *only* page 113.
While you are flipping, be sure
you can see the picture on page 113
and the one on page 115.
If you flip quickly, the two
pictures will start to look like
<u>one</u> *animated* picture.

Don't forget to add
your own sound-effects!

LEFT HAND HERE

Ricky's Robot
Battled Harder.

RIGHT
THUMB
HERE

RIGHT
INDEX
FINGER
HERE

Ricky's Robot
Battled Harder.

FLIP-O-RAMA 5

(pages 117 and 119)

Remember, flip *only* page 117.
While you are flipping, be sure
you can see the picture on page 117
and the one on page 119.
If you flip quickly, the two
pictures will start to look like
<u>one</u> *animated* picture.

Don't forget to add
your own sound-effects!

LEFT HAND HERE

Ricky's Robot
Won the War.

RIGHT
THUMB
HERE

RIGHT
INDEX
FINGER
HERE

Ricky's Robot
Won the War.

CHAPTER 13

Paying for Mistakes

Poor Major Monkey. His Mecha-Monkeys flew home to Mars, and he could not rule the world anymore.

"Boo-hoo-hoo!" cried Major
Monkey. "I've made a big mistake."

"Yes," said Ricky. "And now you
must pay for your mistake!"

Together, the two heroes put
Major Monkey where he belonged:
in the Squeakyville Jail.

"Thank you boys for saving Earth," said the general. "If there's anything we can do to repay you, please let me know!"

Ricky whispered in
his Robot's ear. The Robot
nodded his giant head.

"Well, sir," said Ricky, "we
sure could use a new minivan."

"Alright," said the general.
"How many would you like?"

CHAPTER 14

Heroes

Ricky and his Mighty Robot flew back to the Space Center to meet Ricky's parents.

"Mom! Dad!" cried Ricky. "Look what the general gave us. A brand-new minivan!"

"Wow!" said Ricky's mother.
"We'll race you home!" said
Ricky's father.

So Ricky Ricotta and his Mighty Robot raced the rocket-powered minivan all the way home.

Soon, the whole Ricotta family
was safe at home eating cheese
pizza and drinking root beer.

"Thank you for rescuing each
other today," said Ricky's mother.

"Yes," said Ricky's father,
"and thank you for paying for
your mistake."

"No problem," said Ricky.

"That's what friends are for!"

HOW TO DRAW RICKY

1.

2.

3.

4.

5.

6.

7.

8.

9.

10.

11.

12.

HOW TO DRAW RICKY'S ROBOT

1.

2.

3.

4.

5.

6.

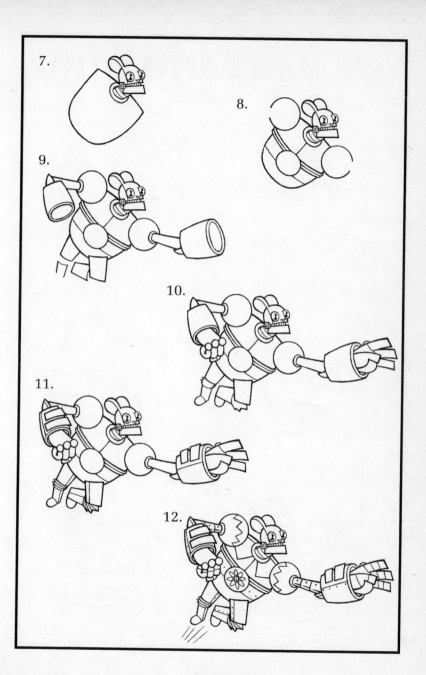

HOW TO DRAW MAJOR MONKEY

1.

2.

3.

4.

5.

6.

HOW TO DRAW A MECHA-MONKEY

1.

2.

3.

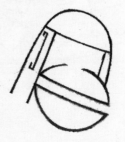

4.

5.

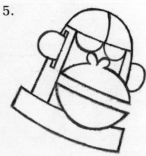

6.

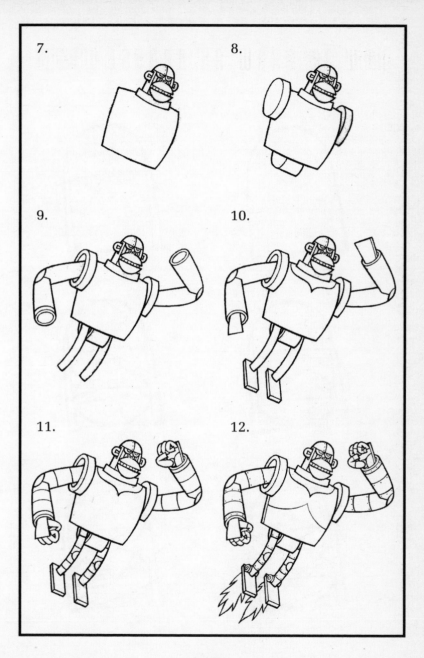

HOW TO DRAW AN ORANGU-TRON

1.

2.

3.

4.

5.

6.

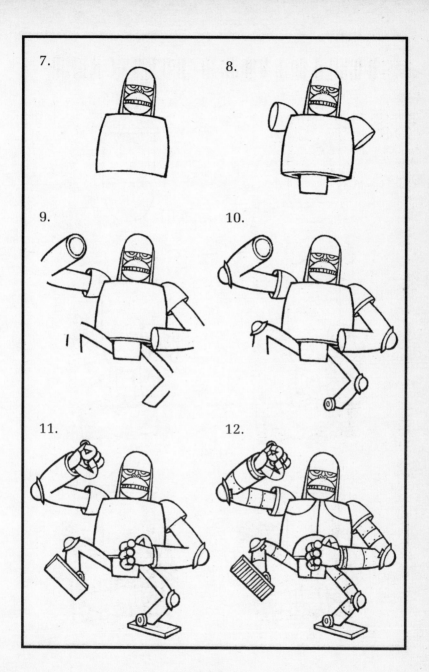

HOW TO DRAW A ROBO-CHIMP

1.

2.

3.

4.

5.

6.

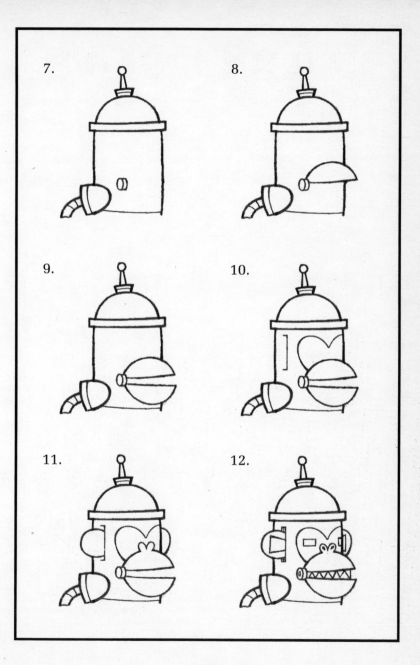

7.

8.

9.

10.

11.

12.

145

Ricky Ricotta's Mighty Robot vs. the Jurassic Jackrabbits from Jupiter

For Joseph and Gracie Ritzert

—D. P.

For Kathy Westray

—M. O.

Chapters

CHAPTER 1

Birthday

One fine morning, Ricky Ricotta woke up and looked at his calendar.

"It's my birthday!" he shouted. "Hooray!"

Ricky ran outside in his pajamas
and woke up his Mighty Robot.

"It's my birthday! It's my birthday!"
shouted Ricky. "This is going to be
the *best* day ever!"

First, Ricky's parents
cooked peanut-butter
pancakes for breakfast.

Then, Ricky's parents gave him
a present.

"Wow! A new bike!" said Ricky.
"Thank you, Mom and Dad!"

Ricky's Mighty Robot did
not have a present for Ricky,
but he had an idea.

The Mighty Robot flew high into the air and spelled out a birthday message in the sky.

"Thank you, Mighty Robot!" said Ricky.

Ricky and his Mighty Robot brushed their teeth and got ready to go to the museum.

"We are going to see real dinosaur skeletons today," said Ricky. "This will be the *BEST* day ever!"

"We have one more surprise for
you," said Ricky's mother. "Your
cousin, Lucy, is coming with us."

"Oh, *NO!*" cried Ricky. "Not
Lucy! She is a little *PEST!*"

"She doesn't mean to be a pest,"
said Ricky's father. "She is just lonely.
She has no friends of her own."

"Now you boys be nice to her," said
Ricky's mother.

"*Rats!*" said Ricky. "This is going
to be the *WORST* day ever!"

CHAPTER 2
General Jackrabbit

Meanwhile, far off in the solar system (about 391 million miles, to be exact), even *worse* things were happening on a huge orange planet called Jupiter.

Jupiter was the largest planet
in the galaxy, and it was orange
because of all the carrots. You see,
Jupiter was the home of billions
of carrot-loving jackrabbits.

But sadly, they were all controlled by an evil ruler named General Jackrabbit.

163

"I will not be happy until I take over all the planets in the galaxy!" said General Jackrabbit. "And I will start with Earth!"

General Jackrabbit and
his two Robo-Rabbit helpers got
into a rocket ship and blasted
off toward Earth.

CHAPTER 3

An Evil Plan

The first thing General Jackrabbit saw when he got to Earth was Ricky Ricotta's Mighty Robot.

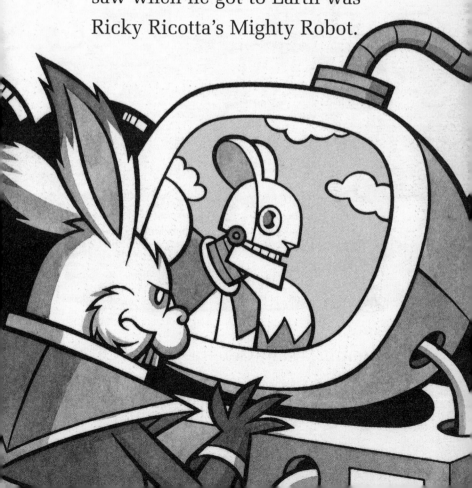

"Hmmm," said General Jackrabbit. "If I want to take over Earth, I'll have to destroy that Mighty Robot first."

Then he got an evil idea.
General Jackrabbit landed
his rocket ship on the roof
of the museum . . .

MUSEUM

. . . and he
sneaked inside.

CHAPTER 4

Lucy the Pest

Meanwhile, Ricky and his family were getting ready to go to the museum. Lucy had just arrived, and she was already being a pest.

"May I have some cake and cookies?" asked Lucy.

"Not until we get back home," said Ricky's mother.

"May I play with the Robot?"
asked Lucy.

"Maybe later," said Ricky's father.

"Will you play princess with me,
Ricky?" asked Lucy.

"No *way*!" said Ricky.

Ricky, Lucy, and Ricky's parents
climbed onto the Mighty Robot's back,
and off they flew to the museum.

"How much longer till we get there?" asked Lucy.

"Soon," said Ricky's father.

"I have to go potty," said Lucy.

"You just went!" said Ricky's mother.

175

"Can we go ice-skating instead of going to the museum?" asked Lucy.

"*You* can," said Ricky, smiling. "We'll drop you off."

Ricky's Mighty Robot giggled.

"*Boys!*" said Ricky's mother. "Be *nice*!"

CHAPTER 5

Museum Mishap

When everyone got to the museum, they noticed that something was not right. The Triceratops looked strange. The Pterodactyl was missing something. And the Tyrannosaurus Rex was all wrong.

"The dinosaurs have lost their heads!" cried the museum guy.

"Don't worry," said Ricky.

"We'll find them!"

Ricky climbed into his Mighty Robot's hand, and the two friends flew off to look for the lost dinosaur heads.

Ricky and his Robot looked all around the museum. But they did not think to look on *TOP* of the museum.

MUSEUM

CHAPTER 6

Send in the Clones

Back on the roof of the museum, General Jackrabbit was doing an evil experiment inside his rocket ship.

He took cells from his three stolen
dinosaur skulls and put them into
his cloning machine. But the
dinosaurs were not complete.
General Jackrabbit needed more
cells. Where could he get them?

"I know," said General Jackrabbit.
"I will add my *own* cells to the
dinosaur cells to make them
complete!" He clipped some hairs
from his fluffy bunny tail and added
them to the dinosaur cells. Suddenly,
the cloning machine began to work.

In a few minutes, three
strange-looking eggs rolled
out of the cloning machine.
"Success at last!" shouted
General Jackrabbit.

Soon the eggs
began to hatch. Out came a
Rabbidactyl, a Trihareatops, and
a Bunnysaurus Rex.

"Perfect!" said General Jackrabbit.

He carried his Jurassic Jackrabbits
up to the nose of his rocket ship and
tossed them out. Then he zapped
them with his Meany Machiney.

ZAAAAAP!

The Jurassic Jackrabbits began to change. They got bigger and bigger, and meaner and meaner.

CHAPTER 7

Jurassic Jack-Attack

Ricky and his Mighty Robot could
not find the dinosaur skulls, so
they flew back to the museum.
There they saw a horrible sight.

"Oh, NO!" cried Ricky.
"Dinosaur Bunnies are
attacking the city!"

The Mighty Robot set Ricky down
near his family. Then the Robot ran
to fight the evil Jurassic Jackrabbits.

The big, bad bunnies had some terrible tricks in store for Ricky's Robot. . . . Like the Crazy Cannonball Creature Crasher . . .

... and an unpleasant pile of Prehistoric Power Punchies!

But Ricky's Robot had some tricks of his own. First came the Electro-Reflecto Ejector Protector.

Then came the Telescopic
Two-Ton Turbo Trasher.

And finally the Forcefully Fearsome Free-Flying Fists of Fury!

The Jurassic Jackrabbits moaned and groaned.

"Get back out there and fight, you dino-dummies," cried General Jackrabbit, "or I'll give you something to moan and groan about."

O-RaMa

HERE'S HOW IT WORKS!

STEP 1
Place your *left* hand inside the dotted lines marked "LEFT HAND HERE." Hold the book open *flat*.

STEP 2
Grasp the *right-hand* page with your right thumb and index finger (inside the dotted lines marked "RIGHT THUMB HERE").

STEP 3
Now *quickly* flip the right-hand page back and forth until the picture appears to be *animated*.

(For extra fun, try adding your own sound-effects!)

FLIP-O-RAMA 1

(pages 207 and 209)

Remember, flip *only* page 207.
While you are flipping, be sure
you can see the picture on page 207
and the one on page 209.
If you flip quickly, the two
pictures will start to look like
<u>one</u> *animated* picture.

Don't forget to add
your own sound-effects!

LEFT HAND HERE

The Jurassic Jackrabbits Attacked.

RIGHT
THUMB
HERE

The Jurassic Jackrabbits Attacked.

FLIP-O-RAMA 2

(pages 211 and 213)

Remember, flip *only* page 211.
While you are flipping, be sure
you can see the picture on page 211
and the one on page 213.
If you flip quickly, the two
pictures will start to look like
<u>one</u> *animated* picture.

Don't forget to add
your own sound-effects!

LEFT HAND HERE

Ricky's Robot Fought Back.

RIGHT
THUMB
HERE

Ricky's Robot
Fought Back.

FLIP-O-RAMA 3

(pages 215 and 217)

Remember, flip *only* page 215.
While you are flipping, be sure
you can see the picture on page 215
and the one on page 217.
If you flip quickly, the two
pictures will start to look like
<u>one</u> *animated* picture.

Don't forget to add
your own sound-effects!

LEFT HAND HERE

The Jurassic Jackrabbits
Battled Hard.

RIGHT
THUMB
HERE

RIGHT
INDEX
FINGER
HERE

The Jurassic Jackrabbits Battled Hard.

FLIP-O-RAMA 4

(pages 219 and 221)

Remember, flip *only* page 219.
While you are flipping, be sure
you can see the picture on page 219
and the one on page 221.
If you flip quickly, the two
pictures will start to look like
<u>one</u> *animated* picture.

Don't forget to add
your own sound-effects!

LEFT HAND HERE

Ricky's Robot
Battled Harder.

RIGHT
THUMB
HERE

Ricky's Robot
Battled Harder.

FLIP-O-RAMA 5

(pages 223 and 225)

Remember, flip *only* page 223.
While you are flipping, be sure
you can see the picture on page 223
and the one on page 225.
If you flip quickly, the two
pictures will start to look like
<u>one</u> *animated* picture.

Don't forget to add
your own sound-effects!

LEFT HAND HERE

Ricky's Robot Won the War.

Ricky's Robot
Won the War.

CHAPTER 9

The Meany Machiney

The Jurassic Jackrabbits had been defeated. But General Jackrabbit was not worried. He just zapped the Jurassic Jackrabbits with *another* blast from his Meany Machiney.

The Jurassic Jackrabbits grew
even *bigger* than before . . . and
much, *much* meaner.

The Jurassic Jackrabbits grabbed Ricky's Mighty Robot in their terrible paws and began laughing and growling.

"I've got to save my Robot!"
cried Ricky. He climbed onto
the roof of the museum and rang
the doorbell on the rocket ship.

Ding-dong.

The two Robo-Rabbits opened
the door.

"No mice allowed!" said the
Robo-Rabbits. "Jackrabbits
ONLY!" Then they slammed
the door in Ricky's face.

"Jackrabbits only, eh?" said
Ricky. Then he got an idea. "I will
need everybody's help today,"
said Ricky. "Especially Lucy's!"

Ricky's family climbed onto
the roof of the museum. Then,
Ricky's mother opened her purse.
She took out two sticks of gum, a
pair of white wool mittens, and
an old white scarf.

Quickly, Ricky's family began
dressing up Lucy. The gum made
great bunny teeth . . .

. . . and the scarf made excellent
bunny ears. And Ricky sewed the
mittens together to make a fluffy tail.

Finally, Lucy climbed onto
Ricky's shoulders.

"Now be careful, you two,"
said Ricky's father.

"Don't worry," said Ricky.
"The good guys always win!"

CHAPTER 10

Ricky and Lucy to the Rescue

Ricky and Lucy went to the rocket ship and rang the doorbell again.

Ding-dong.

When the Robo-Rabbits opened the door this time, they saw a beautiful girl rabbit.

"I'm in love," said the first Robo-Rabbit.

"Ooh-la-laaa!" said the second Robo-Rabbit. "Hubba-hubba!" They took Lucy (and Ricky) into the rocket ship and sat them down at a big table.

"I'm hungry!" said Lucy. "May I
have some cake and pie and cookies
and muffins and cupcakes and
bagels and waffles and doughnuts?"

"Yes, yes, yes!" said the Robo-
Rabbits, and they ran off to start
baking.

"Now is my chance to look around," said Ricky. He crawled out from under the table and sneaked upstairs.

CHAPTER 11

Upstairs

Upstairs, Ricky saw General Jackrabbit with his horrible Meany Machiney.

"Now, Jurassic Jackrabbits, I want you to destroy that Mighty Ro—" General Jackrabbit stopped suddenly and sniffed the air.

Sniff, sniff, sniff.

"Hey!" shouted General Jackrabbit. "Somebody's baking *carrot cake*! What are those silly Robo-Rabbits up to now?"

General Jackrabbit marched
downstairs to see what the problem
was. As soon as he was gone, Ricky
ran to the Meany Machiney and
studied the complex controls.

Ricky turned the dial from BIG,
UGLY 'N' EVIL all the way over to
LITTLE, CUTE 'N' SWEET. Then he
pointed the Meany Machiney at
the Jurassic Jackrabbits.

CHAPTER 12

ZAP!

Downstairs, General Jackrabbit was yelling at his Robo-Rabbits when he heard a loud *ZAP!*

"What's going on up there?" he cried.

General Jackrabbit dashed
upstairs and saw Ricky blasting
the Jurassic Jackrabbits.

ZAP! ZAP! ZAP!

The Jurassic Jackrabbits got littler,
cuter, and sweeter with each zap.

"I'LL GET YOU FOR THIS!"
screamed General Jackrabbit. He
grabbed Ricky by the arm and
would not let go.

Suddenly, Lucy appeared at
the top of the stairs with a
fresh carrot pie.

"Yoo-hoo!" sang Lucy.

General Jackrabbit turned
around and . . .

CHAPTER 13

Ricky's Robot Saves the Day

Ricky's Mighty Robot flew down to the rocket ship to rescue Ricky and Lucy.

"Now we've got to make things right again," said Ricky.

First, Ricky's Robot put the
dinosaur skulls back where they
belonged . . . sort of.

253

Then, Ricky's Robot carefully closed the rocket ship. With one mighty toss, the Robot sent the ship sailing safely back to Jupiter.

"Bye-bye, Robo-Rabbits!"
cried Lucy.

Finally, it was off to jail for
General Jackrabbit.

*"This has been the worst day
ever!"* cried General Jackrabbit.

CHAPTER 14

Friends

Soon Ricky and his family got home.
It was time for pizza and
birthday cake.

"I sure love these cute little Jurassic Jackrabbits," said Lucy.

"Then you should keep them," said Ricky. "Now you'll have little friends of your own!"

"Really?" asked Lucy. "Are you sure you don't want them?"

"I don't need them," said Ricky.
"I already have the biggest friend
in town!"

Finally, Ricky blew out the candles on his cake.

"You know," said Ricky, "this really was the best day ever!"

"Thank you for being so brave today," said Ricky's parents.

"And thank you for sharing," said Lucy.

"No problem," said Ricky . . .

... "that's what friends are for!"

HOW TO DRAW RICKY

1.

2.

3.

4.

5.

6.

7.

8.

9.

10.

11.

12.

HOW TO DRAW RICKY'S ROBOT

1.

2.

3.

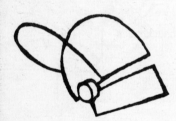

4.

5.

6.

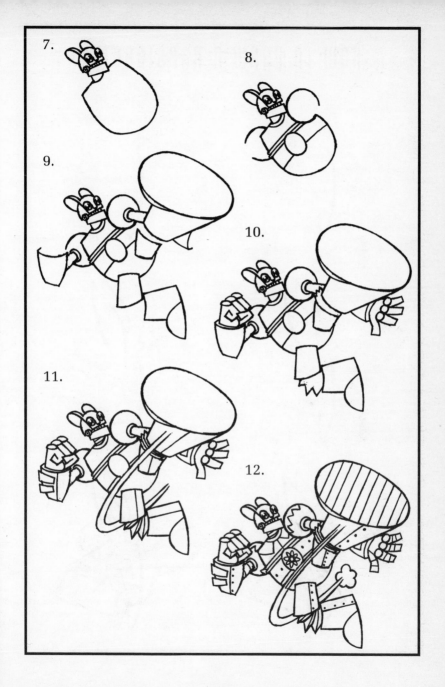

HOW TO DRAW A RABBIDACTYL

1.

2.

3.

4.

5.

6.

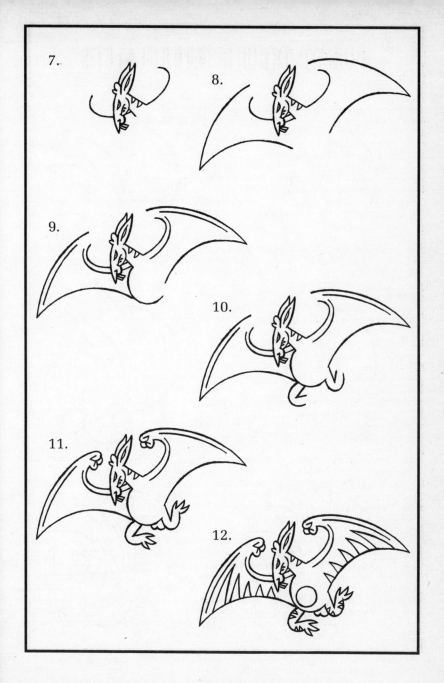

HOW TO DRAW A TRIHAREATOPS

1.

2.

3.

4.

5.

6.

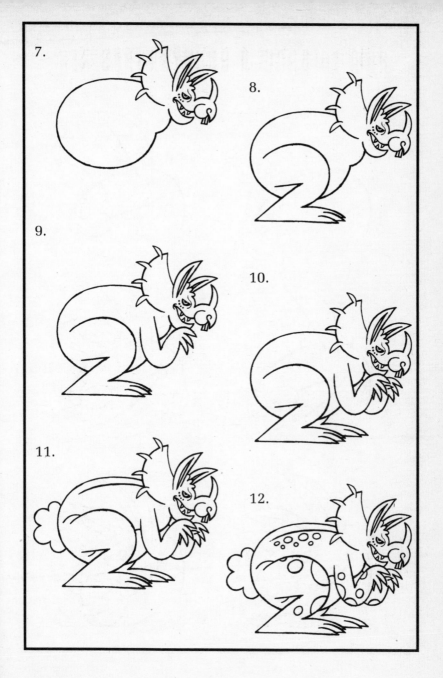

HOW TO DRAW A BUNNYSAURUS REX

1.

2.

3.

4.

5.

6.

Ricky Ricotta's Mighty Robot vs. the Stupid Stinkbugs from Saturn

For Paige Harris Lucas

—D. P.

To Lynn Engstrom, my mentor and friend,

who convinced me to walk the wacky path

of an artist

—M. O.

Chapters

CHAPTER 1

Ricky and his Robot

One fine day, Ricky Ricotta and his Mighty Robot were playing cops and robbers in their yard.

Ricky liked to play the robber because he was good at hiding.

Ricky's Mighty Robot liked playing the cop because he was good at finding things.

"Hey, no fair," Ricky laughed.
"You're not allowed to use
X-ray vision!"

Soon Ricky's mother came outside.

"Come along, boys," she said. "We are going to your cousin Lucy's house for lunch."

"Aww, man!" said Ricky. "Do we *have* to go?"

"Yes," said Ricky's mother. "It will be fun."

"But Uncle Freddie always shakes my hand too hard," said Ricky. "And Auntie Ethel always kisses me too much . . . and Cousin Lucy always wants to play *princess*!"

"Well, we are going anyway," said
Ricky's mother. "So please try to
have some fun."

"We'll go," Ricky sighed, "but we
won't have any fun!"

CHAPTER 2

Uncle Freddie and Auntie Ethel

Soon Ricky and his parents arrived at Cousin Lucy's house.

"Hello, Ricky, my boy," said Uncle Freddie. He grabbed Ricky's hand and shook it hard.

"*Ow!*" said Ricky.

"Come on now," said Uncle Freddie. "Nobody likes a wimpy handshake!"

Auntie Ethel reached down and kissed Ricky all over his face.

"Yuck!" said Ricky.

"Now, now," said Auntie Ethel. "Everybody loves kisses!"

Ricky's Mighty Robot wanted to say
hello, too. He reached down and
shook Uncle Freddie's hand.

"Owza *yowza!*" shouted Uncle
Freddie.

"Nobody likes a wimpy handshake,"
Ricky giggled.

Then Ricky's Robot gave Auntie
Ethel a big, slobbery kiss.

"What's the matter?" Ricky
laughed. "I thought you *loved*
kisses!"

Ricky and his Mighty Robot flew
into the backyard.

There was Lucy, having a tea party
with her pets.

"Wow!" cried Ricky. "Look how big your Jurassic Jackrabbits got!"

"They like to eat," said Lucy. "So I named them Fudgie, Cupcake, and Waffles."

Ricky rolled his eyes.

"Let's play *princess*!" Lucy said.

"No way!" said Ricky.

"Oh, come on," Lucy begged. "I'll be the beautiful princess, and you can be the ugly prince. Fudgie, Cupcake, and Waffles will be our royal ponies, and your Robot can be the big, brave knight."

"What part of *no way* don't you understand?" asked Ricky.

"Now boys," said Ricky's father, "I want you to play nicely with Lucy."

"Rats!" said Ricky. "This is turning out to be a very bad day."

But what Ricky didn't know was that things were about to get much, much worse.

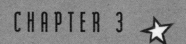

CHAPTER 3

Sergeant Stinkbug

More than 750 million miles away,
there was a polluted planet called
Saturn, which was overrun
with stupid, smelly
stinkbugs.

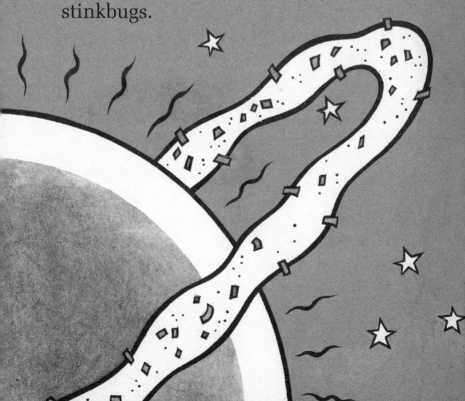

Everywhere you looked, trash filled
the streets . . .

. . . garbage gunked up the rivers . . .

. . . and the factories puffed out so much pollution, it formed a toxic ring of smoke around the whole planet.

But of all the stupid, smelly creatures on Saturn, there was no one stupider or smellier than evil Sergeant Stinkbug. He was the ruler of Saturn, and he was the worst litterbug of all.

Every day when Sergeant Stinkbug was done eating, he threw his dirty dishes out the window.

Every night when he was through
watching his favorite shows, he
tossed his TV out the window.

And every morning when he was
finished sleeping in his bed . . .
well, you get the idea.

Usually, Sergeant Stinkbug loved his smelly, toxic planet. But today as he strolled through Pollution Parkway, he got fed up.

"This place is a DUMP!" he shouted.

"I want to find a new planet that I can junk up!"

So Sergeant Stinkbug gathered
his stinky subjects, climbed aboard
his Giant Spaceship, and headed
for Earth.

CHAPTER 4

The Princess of Earth

When the Giant Spaceship reached Earth, Sergeant Stinkbug spoke to his armies.

"Listen up, you stinkers," said the evil Sergeant. "First we must find the king of Earth and kidnap him. Then we will take over the planet!"

The Stupid Stinkbugs searched
through their Super-Sonic Spy
Scope, but they could not find a
king. They looked all over Earth,
but they couldn't even find a queen.

"Duh, look!" said one of the
Stupid Stinkbugs finally. "I think I
see a princess!"

The Super-Sonic Spy Scope zoomed in on Lucy, who was standing on the picnic table giving orders.

"You guys have to protect me," Lucy said, "so the bad guys don't steal all of my precious rubies!"

"A-*HA*!" cried Sergeant Stinkbug.
"I'll kidnap that princess and steal all
of those rubies she was talking about.
Then we'll all take over the planet!"

So Sergeant Stinkbug got into his
Attack Pod and headed for Lucy's
house.

CHAPTER 5

The Picnic

Soon it was time for lunch. Ricky's
aunt and uncle brought food out to
everybody. Then they went back
inside to eat with Ricky's parents.

Fudgie, Cupcake, Waffles, Ricky, and his Mighty Robot all dove into their grilled cheese sandwiches.

"C'mon you guys," Lucy whined. "Let's play *before* we eat."

Suddenly, Sergeant Stinkbug
showed up. He lowered the
Automatic Snatcher Arm on his
Attack Pod and grabbed Lucy.

"Hey, look everybody," cried Lucy. "A bad guy is trying to steal my rubies!"

"Yeah, *right*," said Ricky, who didn't even bother to turn around.

"C'mon you guys!" cried Lucy. "Stop eating and save me from this evil space-bug!"

"Boy," said Ricky, "that kid sure has a vivid imagination."

CHAPTER 6

Lucy in the Sky with Rubies

Sergeant Stinkbug carried Lucy high into the air and demanded to know where all the rubies were.

"They're right here on my crown, you big dummy!" said Lucy.

"Those aren't real," said Sergeant
Stinkbug. "You just drew those on
with crayons!"

"You better put me down before
my Jurassic Jackrabbits beat you up!"
said Lucy.

"Ooh! I'm *so scared*!" mocked Sergeant Stinkbug. "Did you draw *them* with crayons, too?"

"No," said Lucy. "They're *real* . . .

. . . and they're right behind you!"

Sergeant Stinkbug turned and saw Fudgie, Cupcake, and Waffles.

"Help!" he screamed. The Automatic Snatcher Arm let go of Lucy and she fell . . .

. . . right into the Mighty Robot's hand.

"Nice catch!" said Lucy.

Ricky's Mighty Robot grabbed Sergeant Stinkbug's Attack Pod and held it tightly.

"Alright," said Ricky, "what's going on here?"

"Ooh, nothing," said Sergeant Stinkbug, as he reached down and pushed the EMERGENCY ATTACK button on his wristwatch.

Suddenly, the Giant Spaceship floating above Earth opened up. Two Warrior Stinkbugs flew out of the spaceship and down to Sergeant Stinkbug's side. They were ready to attack.

CHAPTER 7

The Big Fight

Sergeant Stinkbug reached into a bag
and grabbed two round gumballs.

"My Grow-Big Gumballs should do
the trick," laughed the evil Sergeant.
"Here you go, my uglies!"

He threw the gumballs into the
Warrior Stinkbugs' mouths.

The Warriors chewed and chewed, and they grew bigger and bigger and bigger. Then they attacked Ricky's Robot.

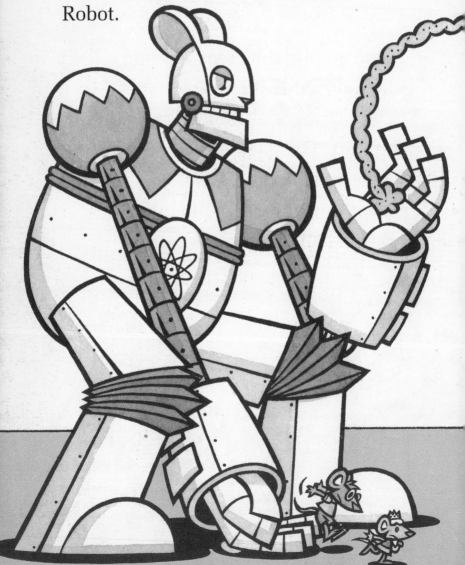

321

The Stupid Stinkbugs started their assault with a super-smashin' swinger stomp.

But Ricky's Robot bounced back
with a bone-bustin' blast from
his bionic belt buckle.

Then he finished his fight
for freedom with a free-flyin'
foot in their funky faces.

CHAPTER 8

Captured

Ricky's Mighty Robot was victorious, but not for long. Sergeant Stinkbug leaned out of his Attack Pod and tossed more Grow-Big Gumballs into the mouths of his Warrior Stinkbugs.

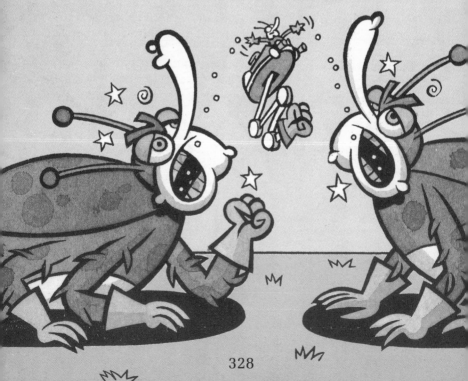

As the Warriors chewed, they grew
and grew and grew some more.

Soon the Warriors were ten times bigger than Ricky's Mighty Robot. They grabbed Ricky's Robot in their gigantic fists and prepared to pound him to pieces.

"We've got to save my Robot!"
cried Ricky.

Together, Ricky, Lucy, and Waffles
worked out a plan.

Fudgie and Cupcake wanted to
help, too, but they couldn't fly.

"You boys just stay here and think good thoughts!" said Lucy, kissing them on their noses. "We'll be back soon, and everything will be fine!"

Ricky, Lucy, and Waffles flew up to Sergeant Stinkbug's Attack Pod.

"Let go of my Robot right now," yelled Ricky, "or you'll be sorry!"

"You're the one who's going to be sorry," laughed Sergeant Stinkbug. He pressed a button on his ship and sprayed our three heroes with Super-Stenchy Stink-Gas.

The Automatic Snatcher Arm reached out, grabbed Ricky, Lucy, and Waffles, and held them tightly. Then Sergeant Stinkbug called for his troops.

The Giant Spaceship opened up.
Suddenly, hundreds of Attack Pods
poured out, lining up in formation.

CHAPTER 9

Fudgie and Cupcake to the Rescue

Fudgie and Cupcake watched the horror unfold above their heads. It looked like the end of the world. They knew they couldn't fly, but they still had to do *something*.

So Fudgie and Cupcake ran up the
leg of one of the Warrior Stinkbugs.
They dashed across his thigh, then
bolted up his back.

Finally, the two Jurassic Jackrabbits
scurried up to the Warrior Stinkbug's
shoulder and jumped.

Down they fell until they crash-
landed on Sergeant Stinkbug's
Attack Pod.

The collision caused Sergeant
Stinkbug to flip out of his Pod, but
Cupcake caught him.

"Hooray for Fudgie and Cupcake!"
shouted Ricky and Lucy.

Fudgie rummaged through the Attack Pod until he found the Grow-Big Gumballs.

"Good boy, Fudgie!" said Ricky. "Now toss 'em here!"

Fudgie wagged his fluffy tail and dropped the bag of gumballs into Ricky's hands. Ricky popped six gumballs into his mouth, then chewed and chewed . . .

. . . and grew and grew and grew!

Now Ricky was as big as the Warrior Stinkbugs. He grabbed his Mighty Robot out of their hands and tucked him into his shirt pocket.

"Don't worry, Mighty Robot," said Ricky, "it's *my* turn to save the day!"

CHAPTER 10

The Big Battle

(IN FLIP-O-RAMA™)

ꓷ-RaMa

HERE'S HOW IT WORKS!

STEP 1

Place your *left* hand inside the dotted lines marked "LEFT HAND HERE." Hold the book open *flat*.

STEP 2

Grasp the *right-hand* page with your right thumb and index finger (inside the dotted lines marked "RIGHT THUMB HERE").

STEP 3

Now *quickly* flip the right-hand page back and forth until the picture appears to be *animated*.

(For extra fun, try adding your own sound-effects!)

FLIP-O-RAMA 1

(pages 351 and 353)

Remember, flip *only* page 351.
While you are flipping, be sure
you can see the picture on page 351
and the one on page 353.
If you flip quickly, the two
pictures will start to look like
<u>one</u> *animated* picture.

Don't forget to add
your own sound-effects!

LEFT HAND HERE

The Stupid Stinkbugs Attacked.

RIGHT
THUMB
HERE

The Stupid Stinkbugs
Attacked.

FLIP-O-RAMA 2

(pages 355 and 357)

Remember, flip *only* page 355.
While you are flipping, be sure
you can see the picture on page 355
and the one on page 357.
If you flip quickly, the two
pictures will start to look like
<u>one</u> *animated* picture.

Don't forget to add
your own sound-effects!

LEFT HAND HERE

Ricky Fought Back.

Ricky Fought Back.

FLIP-O-RAMA 3

(pages 359 and 361)

Remember, flip *only* page 359.
While you are flipping, be sure
you can see the picture on page 359
and the one on page 361.
If you flip quickly, the two
pictures will start to look like
<u>one</u> *animated* picture.

Don't forget to add
your own sound-effects!

LEFT HAND HERE

The Stupid Stinkbugs
Battled Hard.

RIGHT
THUMB
HERE

The Stupid Stinkbugs
Battled Hard.

FLIP-O-RAMA 4

(pages 363 and 365)

Remember, flip *only* page 363.
While you are flipping, be sure
you can see the picture on page 363
and the one on page 365.
If you flip quickly, the two
pictures will start to look like
<u>one</u> *animated* picture.

Don't forget to add
your own sound-effects!

LEFT HAND HERE

Ricky Battled Harder.

Ricky Battled Harder.

FLIP-O-RAMA 5

(pages 367 and 369)

Remember, flip *only* page 367.
While you are flipping, be sure
you can see the picture on page 367
and the one on page 369.
If you flip quickly, the two
pictures will start to look like
<u>one</u> *animated* picture.

Don't forget to add
your own sound-effects!

LEFT HAND HERE

Ricky Ricotta
Won the War.

RIGHT
THUMB
HERE

Ricky Ricotta Won the War.

CHAPTER 11

The Final Attack

Ricky had won his battle with the giant Warrior Stinkbugs.

But Sergeant Stinkbug still had one more trick up his sleeve.

He pressed a button on his wrist-watch and called for his Attack Pod Troops to attack.

Suddenly, hundreds of Attack Pods started zooming toward Earth.

"Oh, NO!" cried Ricky. "There are too many of them! How will I ever stop them all?"

Just then, a giant finger emerged from a cloud and tapped Ricky on his shoulder. It was Lucy. She had chewed up the rest of the bag of gumballs when nobody was looking.

"I couldn't help it," said Lucy. "I *love* gumballs!"

Lucy reached into outer space
and opened up the Giant Spaceship.
With it, she scooped up all of the
tiny Attack Pods. Then she shoved
the two Warrior Stinkbugs inside.

CHAPTER 12

Just Desserts

Fudgie and Waffles found a bag of Super-Shrinking Saltwater Taffy inside Sergeant Stinkbug's Attack Pod.

They gave the bag to Ricky's Robot, and he fed it to Ricky and Lucy.

Soon, the two cousins had shrunk
back to their normal sizes.

Together, the six friends flew
Sergeant Stinkbug to the
Squeakyville Jail.

Then they zoomed back to Lucy's house just in time for dessert.

The grown-ups brought out big slices of chocolate-chip cheesecake for everybody.

"We heard loud noises out here,"
said Auntie Ethel.

"What have you kids been up to?"
asked Uncle Freddie.

"Well, a bad guy tried to steal my
rubies," said Lucy, "but Ricky's Robot
beat up the Stinkbugs. Then Fudgie
found some gum and I grew big and
clobbered the Attack Pods and . . . "

"Boy," said Ricky's mother, "those
kids sure have vivid imaginations!"

"I know that Lucy gets on your nerves sometimes," Ricky's dad whispered, "but thank you for being nice to her anyway."

"No problem," said Ricky . . .

... "that's what friends are for!"

HOW TO DRAW RICKY

1.

2.

3.

4.

5.

6.

7.

8.

9.

10.

11.

12.

HOW TO DRAW RICKY'S ROBOT

1.

2.

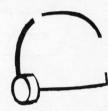

3.

4.

5.

6.

HOW TO DRAW LUCY

1.

2.

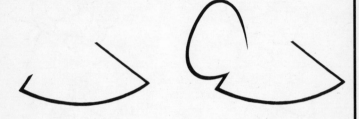

3.

4.

5.

6.

7.

8.

9.

10.

11.

12.

HOW TO DRAW SERGEANT STINKBUG

1.

2.

3.

4.

5.

6.

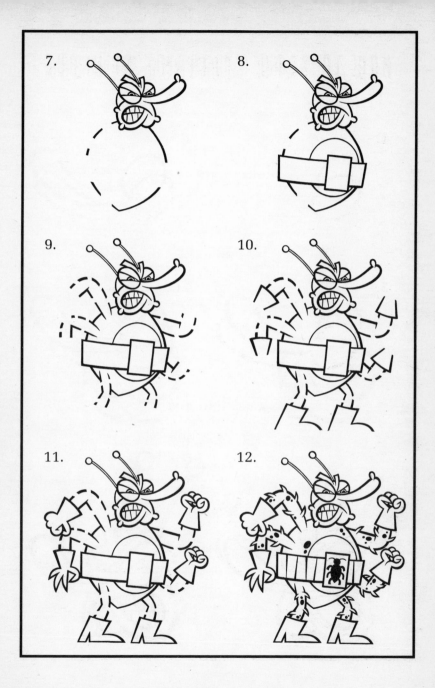

HOW TO DRAW A WARRIOR STINKBUG

1.

2.

3.

4.

5.

6.

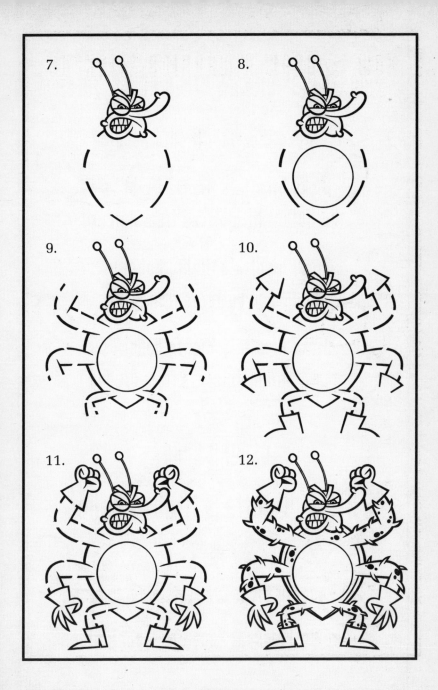

DON'T MISS RICKY'S OTHER ADVENTURES:

Ricky Ricotta's Mighty Robot

Ricky Ricotta's Mighty Robot vs.
the Mutant Mosquitoes from Mercury

Ricky Ricotta's Mighty Robot vs.
the Voodoo Vultures from Venus

Ricky Ricotta's Mighty Robot vs.
the Uranium Unicorns from Uranus

COMING SOON:

Ricky Ricotta's Mighty Robot

vs.

The Naughty Night Crawlers from Neptune

The Un-Pleasant Penguins from Pluto

About the Author and Illustrator

DAV PILKEY created his first stories as comic books while he was in elementary school. In 1997, he wrote and illustrated his first adventure novel for children, *The Adventures of Captain Underpants*, which received rave reviews and was an instant bestseller—as were all the books that followed in the series. Dav is also the creator of numerous award-winning picture books, including *The Paperboy*, a Caldecott Honor Book, and the Dumb Bunnies books. He and his dog live in Eugene, Oregon.

It was a stroke of luck when Dav discovered the work of artist **MARTIN ONTIVEROS**. Dav knew that Martin was just the right illustrator for the Ricky Ricotta's Mighty Robot series. Martin has loved drawing since he was a kid. He lives in Portland, Oregon. He has a lot of toys, which he shares with his young son, Felix.